The Canterville Ghost

WRITTEN BY OSCAR WILDE

Adapted by Caroline Castle

Illustrated by Mario Coelho

OXFORD
UNIVERSITY PRESS

OXFORD
UNIVERSITY PRESS

is a department of the University of Oxford.
It furthers the University's objective of excellence in research, scholarship,
and education by publishing worldwide in

Oxford   New York

Auckland   Cape Town   Dar es Salaam   Hong Kong   Karachi
Kuala Lumpur   Madrid   Melbourne   Mexico City   Nairobi
New Delhi   Shanghai   Taipei   Toronto

With offices in

Argentina   Austria   Brazil   Chile   Czech Republic   France   Greece
Guatemala   Hungary   Italy   Japan   Poland   Portugal   Singapore
South Korea   Switzerland   Thailand   Turkey   Ukraine   Vietnam

Oxford is a registered trade mark of Oxford University Press
in the UK and in certain other countries

British Library Cataloguing in Publication Data

Data available

ISBN: 978-0-19-911760-4

10 9 8 7 6 5 4 3 2

Cover illustration by Anne Jewett

Inside illustrations by Mario Coelho

Printed in China by Imago

Paper used in the production of this book is a natural, recyclable product
made from wood grown in sustainable forests. The manufacturing process
conforms to the environmental regulations of the country of origin.

Contents

CHAPTER I

The bloodstain on the floor

The house was very big. To the Otis family, who had just arrived in England from America, it also seemed very old. However, it wasn't until they stepped out of the carriage* that they saw how big it was. They had to crane their necks backwards to take it all in.

'Wow!' said Virginia Otis, the only girl in the family. She thought it was the grandest thing she had ever seen.

'Doesn't look haunted to me!' said twin one, Georgie.

'Nor to me!' said twin two, Harry.

'Parrot!' said twin one.

'It's all rubbish, this ghost stuff,' said their older brother, Washington. 'They think we Americans will believe anything.'

Canterville Chase was the name of their new home. Mr Otis had bought it from old Lord Canterville whose family had lived there for hundreds of years. Oddly, he had warned Mr Otis against buying it. He said the Cantervilles had been 'haunted out of house and home'. There was supposed to be a three-hundred-year-old ghost flitting around at night and scaring people out of their wits.

Mrs Otis had just laughed. 'We'll buy the house and everything inside it, and that includes any ghosts!' she'd said. Everyone thought they were completely mad.

Virginia sort of agreed too, but for different reasons. To be honest, she wouldn't have minded a ghost. The house was miles from anywhere. She could see months, even years, of boredom ahead. A ghost would liven things up a bit. Although when they arrived, it wasn't ghostly weather at all. It was a hot, sunny day in the middle of July.

But as they began lugging their suitcases to the huge front door something strange happened. Everything went dark! Not midnight dark, but all misty and grey. Then a flock of big, black birds flew overhead. The Otis family were stunned into silence.

'Crows,' said Mr Otis.

'*A flock of crows,*
a bleak storm blows,'*
said a voice from the steps.

They looked up. An old lady was standing by the door. She was dressed all in black with a white cap and apron.

'I bid you welcome,' she said in a funny, old-fashioned voice. 'I am Mrs Umney, the housekeeper.'*

She hurried them inside. They passed, single file, through a huge hall and into the library. This was a long, low room, panelled with black oak. At the end was a stained glass window.

For some reason, everyone was quiet (even the twins). They sat down on the big, old sofas while Mrs Umney served tea from an ancient-looking silver teapot. It looked none too hygienic.

Mrs Otis was staring at the floor, just by the fireplace. 'Oh dear,' she said. 'Look. Something has been spilled there.'

Mrs Umney glanced down. '*Blood* has been spilled on that spot,' she said.

'Ooo, how horrible!' said Mrs Otis, clasping her chest. 'We don't want any *blood* on our floor. It must be cleared up at once.'

Mrs Umney gave a funny grin. More like a grimace, really.

'It is the blood of Lady Eleanor de Canterville,' she said in a raspy voice. 'Poor woman. She was killed on that very same spot by her husband, Sir Simon. The year was

1575.* Later, Sir Simon disappeared. He didn't even leave a note.'

She glared around the room as if expecting Sir Simon to come leaping out of the panelling at any second. 'His body has never been found. But his guilty ghost still haunts this house. Mark my words, Mrs Otis.'

'Poppycock!'* cried Washington, leaping to his feet. 'Complete rubbish. If you'd get me some Potts' Clean-Away,* I'll clear it up in a jiffy.'

'I wouldn't do that, sir,' said Mrs Umney in gloomy tones.

'I'll get it myself,' said Washington. A few minutes later he was back, and down on his hands and knees, scrubbing away.

Mrs Umney looked terrified. 'What are you doing?' she cried.

'Look! I told you,' said Washington proudly. He lifted the cloth. 'All gone!'

Just then something else strange happened. The whole room went stark white! Then there was a sudden, bone-shaking peal of thunder. Everyone leaped up, except Mrs Umney. She *fainted*. Worst of all, Georgie disappeared!

'Oh, my goodness,' cried Mrs Otis. 'Georgie, dear boy. Where are you?'

For a moment, even Mr Otis and Washington believed that something ghostly and ghastly had happened to twin one. Then they heard a muffled voice. It was coming from Mrs Umney. 'Help! Help!'

A small, pale hand seemed to poke out from her left side.

'Heavens!' cried Mrs Otis. 'What is happening?'

Mr Otis helped Mrs Umney up from the floor, and Washington fanned her with a newspaper.

To everyone's relief, there was Georgie. A bit flattened, but all in one piece.

'Well!' said Mrs Otis. 'What an eventful start.' And after making sure both Mrs Umney and Georgie were unhurt, she suggested that the family should go up to their rooms.

Mrs Umney was not happy.

'You shouldn't have done that, Mr Washington,' she said. 'That blood has been there for centuries. Who *knows* what will happen now? I have seen things with my own eyes. Many a night I dare not even lay down my head for fear of the terrible things that go on.'

'Don't worry about that, dear,' said Mrs Otis. 'We Otises are not afraid of ghosts. I can promise you.'

Up in the highest part of the house, there was a horrid peal of laughter. It was Sir Simon de Canterville, the Canterville Ghost. Luckily he was too far away for the Otis family to hear.

'*"Not afraid of ghosts!"* We'll see about *that*,'

he scoffed. '*Oh*, yes! Americans too. Should be a piece of cake, as they say these days.'

CHAPTER 2

High spirits

Virginia didn't feel at all afraid, even though a big storm blew up. She had a cosy little room at the top of the main stairs, and she slept right through the night.

But when she went down for breakfast the next morning, everyone was crowded round the fireplace in the library, staring at something.

'The stain is back!' cried Georgie.

'It's back!' cried Harry.

'It can't be,' said Washington. 'Potts' never fails.'

'Must be the g-h-o-s-t. Oooo!' hissed

Georgie, rushing around waving his arms.

'It's the ghost!' cried Harry, doing the same.

'Stop copying me!' screamed Georgie.

'Boys, boys!' said Mrs Otis calmly. 'Please be quiet. If we don't have a ghost now, we soon will. You're making enough noise to wake the dead.'

Washington started madly scrubbing at the stain again. 'There,' he said. 'Gone. That should put an end to it.'

That night Mr Otis locked the library, just to be on the safe side.

But in the morning, there was another surprise. The stain was back.

'Hmm,' said Mr Otis. 'I must say this is most odd. Perhaps there is something to Mrs Umney's story after all.'

'Well, maybe and maybe not,' said Mother. 'Let's not worry our heads about it. Look outside – it's a lovely day. Let's all go out for a nice drive.'

So off they went in the carriage. The roads were tiny and everything was wonderfully

green. Virginia began to think she liked
England after all. It was a blazing hot day and
she sang a little song as they trotted on.

Someone on horseback came past, and Mr
Otis stopped the carriage to say good morning.
The young rider looked about the same age as
Washington, so the Otis family were amazed
when he said he was the Duke of Cheshire!

Mr Otis invited him over for tea the following week.

They arrived home in high spirits, all thoughts of ghosts and hauntings quite forgotten.

Washington was playing tag with the twins.

Virginia was humming a new song and thinking how grand the house looked in the sunlight.

And then something odd happened. All the windows in the house seemed to black out! The Otises looked at each other. What was going on?

Sir Simon de Canterville, the Canterville Ghost, watched them get out of their carriage.

'All very jolly and full of the joys of summer,' he muttered.

'*Chat, chat, chat. Twitter, twitter, twitter.* Who do they think they are? *"We Otises are not afraid of ghosts!"* Oh, *really*? I know they weren't that bothered by the bloodstain and the storm. But those were just starters. Tasters, really.'

Now it was time to get down to serious haunting.

CHAPTER 3

―◆◆◆―

Potts' All-Purpose Oil

The Otis family went to bed early. By eleven o'clock they were all tucked up and fast asleep. Sir Simon looked out of a window at the top of Canterville Chase and smiled a ghostly smile. Conditions were perfect. Dense fog and no moon.

He put on one of his favourite haunting outfits and glided silently down the stairs to the first floor. Once in the hall, he let his feet clank to the ground.

Catching sight of himself in the mirror, he admired the effect: eyes as red as burning coals, long, straggly hair, and jingling chains hanging from his wrists. Rusty chains round his ankles rasped along the floorboards. These Otises, who were 'not afraid of ghosts', were in for a big shock.

Sir Simon decided to start with Mr Otis. Once he'd scared him out of his wits, the rest of the family would be *terrified*. In front of him, faint candlelight oozed from underneath a door. *Stomp, stomp, stomp*. He clanked towards it. There was the rattle of a doorknob as the door opened.

'My dear man! Haven't you heard of *oil*? We really cannot have rusty chains clunking around all night. You'll wake the whole house!'

The ghost stopped, amazed. In front of him was Mr Hiram Otis. He was standing in the doorway in his dressing gown holding out a little bottle.

The ghost drew himself up to his full height. Jangling his chains, he gave the most horrible moan. 'AAAAGH!'

Mr Otis pushed the bottle towards Sir Simon.

'My dear sir, don't get upset! This is Potts' All-Purpose Oil. I use it for my hair, but it will work just as well for rusty chains.'

Sir Simon was too shocked even to rattle his bones. Didn't this man know who he was?

'Here,' said Mr Otis, 'I'll put the oil on the table by the candles. Help yourself.'

Did this American have no respect? Sir Simon swiped the bottle to the ground in a fury. Then, clanking his chains, he turned and fled.

But it was not over. As he rounded the corner, two small creatures dressed in white burst out of a doorway, yelling their heads off. A large pillow whizzed by, just missing his head. Those horrible twins! Had they no fear?

Back in his secret room, Sir Simon fell against the wall and *fumed*. Red-hot steam hissed from his ears like smoke. Never in his brilliant career had he been so angry. People were usually *petrified*. What was he doing wrong? He thought over some of his past successes.

1 Grinning through the curtains during a storm. This had made four housemaids faint in one go!

2 Old 'Nosy Bones'. Madame* Tremour had been terrified when she awoke to find his skeleton sitting in her armchair reading her diary!

3 The green hand tapping at the window. This had made the head butler* lock himself in the pantry* for a week.

4 Skeleton skittles. Everyone had shrieked in terror as he played skittles with his own bones on the front lawn. Genius!

And now some silly American was offering him Potts' All-Purpose Oil! Unbearable! No ghost in history had been treated in this way.

He was sure of that. He spent the rest of the
night in deep thought. He needed a new plan
of action.

CHAPTER 4

The big idea

The Otis family were all at breakfast, talking about the ghost. 'I am annoyed', said Mr Otis, 'that he didn't accept my little gift. Ungrateful fellow!'

'How rude!' said Georgie.

'Very rude!' said Harry.

'Well, it wasn't very *polite* to throw pillows at him,' said Virginia.

'I don't wish the fellow any harm,' said Mr Otis, 'but we can't have chains clanking around all night. We really can't.'

Breakfast over, everyone trooped into the library to find Mrs Umney standing by the fireplace. She pointed to the floor and said,

'*Leave what you find well alone,*
or trouble will surely visit this home.'

'I do not believe it!' said Washington. 'It's *back.*'

They all looked on the floor. There was the stain again. This time it was more purple than red.

'Very odd,' said Mrs Otis. 'Very odd indeed.'

And for the rest of that week, the stain kept coming back. Every day Washington would clean it up, and every morning it would be there again. Even stranger, the colour kept changing. On the third morning it was a dull red. On the fourth morning it was a sort of orange. Then on the fifth day it was purple again, and on Saturday a vivid *green*!

At this point Virginia began to wonder.
Something was beginning to fall into place.

◆◆◆

Up in his room, Sir Simon was also thinking
things over. He was getting bored with the
bloodstain. He had been waiting for a really
good idea. And on Sunday it came. THE BIG
ONE. He grinned to himself. There'd be no
more 'My dear fellows' and no more 'Potts'
All-Purpose Anything'. If the family weren't
driven out of their wits and on the boat back*
to the USA within the week – he'd give up
haunting for ever. He set to work immediately.

It was the dead of night. As soon as he was sure they were all sleeping, he flitted down to the big hall. There it was. The magnificent suit of armour worn by Sir Archibald Canterville in the battle of Biggins Bulge* in 1494. And what a fearsome thing it was! It had a helmet from which his piercing red eyes would gleam like fire, a jagged battle-axe* and horrible spiked ball and chain.*

He chuckled to himself. When the Otis family saw this lot clunking towards them, they'd wish they'd never been born, let alone set foot in Canterville Chase.

He crept up to it ever so carefully. But then he slipped and stumbled. There was an awful creaking noise, then OUCH! The whole clanking lot fell on top of him!

Sir Simon dragged himself out from under half a ton of heavy steel. His knees were grazed and his foot hurt horribly.

Then there they were! Mr Hiram Otis and his three awful sons in their nightclothes. The older boy held up a candle. They were staring

at him as if they just *hadn't* seen a ghost.

Then: ping! ping! ping! ping! Those hateful twins were firing peashooters!*

Mr Otis stepped forward. 'Sir!' he cried. 'Hold up your hands and surrender!'

Surrender? *Him*? The Canterville Ghost! Sir Simon was stunned. This was the final straw. He shrieked with rage and swept like a whirlwind up the stairs, blowing out Washington's candle as he did so.

By the time he reached the top of the stairs, his foot was hurting like mad. But he had one last secret weapon. His ghastly cackle. (He had always had great success with this. He once turned a baronet's* hair from black to white in a single second.)

He took a deep breath and laughed his most horrible laugh. The old hall rang and rang again with its fearful echo.

A door opened and there was Mrs Otis, standing in a fluffy, blue dressing gown. She held out another bottle. 'Poor chap! You don't sound well at all,' she said. 'Here, take this. It's

Potts' Cure-All Syrup. It works for everything from tummy ache to sore throats. Take two spoonfuls before you go to bed. By morning you'll be as right as rain.'

Sir Simon was beside himself with rage. What would it take to prove to these Otises that they had a real, one hundred per cent spook under their noses? But then he heard the clatter of footsteps on the stairs. The pinging of peashooters was getting nearer. He fled.

Back in his room, Sir Simon broke down and cried. Those dreadful twins, they couldn't be more than nine. He was three hundred and *ninety-nine*! No respect at all for their elders. And the rest of them with their candles and Potts'-this and Potts'-that.

But the worst thing, the absolute worst thing, was that he hadn't been able to wear the suit of armour. He had been *so* looking forward to that.

He spent the next three days recovering, getting up only to put back the stain in the library.

But he had already started on his next plan...

CHAPTER 5

Tea with the duke

Virginia had slept peacefully through all the excitement. So she was rather taken aback at breakfast when the tale was told.

The twins were full of themselves. Georgie stood up and made silly pinging noises with an imaginary peashooter.

'*I* got him!' yelled Harry. 'I got him right on the nose.'

'No, you didn't!' cried Georgie. 'It was *me*!'

'Boys, boys,' sighed their mother. 'Sit down and finish your porridge. The poor chap didn't look well, I must say. You're being too hard on him. After all, he has lived at Canterville

Chase a lot longer than we have.'

'I'm *fed up* with this,' came a voice from the library. 'And we're running out of Potts' Clean-Away!'

It was Washington, down on his knees getting rid of that morning's bloodstain. It was a muddy brown. Somehow, Virginia wasn't surprised.

'Now, let's stop talking about ghosts,' said Mrs Otis. 'Have you forgotten? That young Duke of Cheshire and two of his friends are coming over this afternoon.'

Mrs Umney had been listening to every word.

Virginia wondered if she had heard the goings-on last night. Judging by the dark shadows under her eyes, she hadn't slept

a wink. The housekeeper cast her fishy glare
around the table.

'*He who meddles with things not proper,*
mark my words will come a cropper,'
she intoned in a low, rasping voice.

She was not pleased when both twins burst
into howls of laughter.

After lunch, Virginia went out for a trot round the lanes on her pony. It was a lovely sunny day and on the way home, she met the young Duke of Cheshire and his friends on their way to Canterville Chase. They all travelled together and had a wonderful afternoon playing croquet.* The Duke of Cheshire didn't even seem to mind that Washington won all five games. At tea, Virginia sat next to the duke and the rest of the day flew past, all thoughts of ghosts well and truly forgotten.

CHAPTER 6

The King of Ghosts

Sir Simon had not forgotten the Otises,
however. He had chosen Friday 14th August
for his master plan.

And what a plan it was!

His first victim was to be Master Washington
Otis. He'd had quite enough of him and his
Potts' Clean-Away. He would *LOOM* over
the silly boy from the end of his bed, his
arms outstretched while making a noise like
gnashing teeth. Genius.

After putting this foolish young man into a
state of quivering terror, he'd go to victims two
and three.

His plan for Mr and Mrs Otis was to place a clammy claw on Mrs Otis's forehead, while hissing evil tales of long-dead villains in her husband's ear.

Next would be those hateful twins. They deserved a good lesson, the very best he could do.

He would creep between their beds, icy-green and gruesome, and wake them with a fiendish cackle. Then they would watch terror-struck, as he threw off his cloak and crawled around the room, one eyeball glaring horribly and his bones shining white in the moonlight.

Virginia, he did not have a lot against, as she hadn't caused him much trouble. He settled on a few hollow groans from the cupboard, and maybe just a little icy wind and twitching of curtains.

Finally, just to show off, he decided to have some fun with the housekeeper, Mrs Umney. He settled on an old favourite: the flying chamber pot.* He giggled to himself at the idea.

He chose his outfit with great care:
1 A large black hat with a red plume*
2 Clammy, rotting shirt frilled at wrists and
   neck
3 A rusty dagger.

The night was perfect. A violent storm came
on, and the wind was so fierce it rattled every
door and window. The old house shook on its
foundations.

At half-past ten the family went to bed.
At first, the twins kept Sir Simon waiting by
giggling and shrieking.

But when midnight rang out on the hall
clock, all was silent except for a screech owl* in
the old yew tree and the wind moaning around
the house.

Above the wind and rain came the heavy
snoring of Mr Otis. The whole family was fast
asleep.

Sir Simon oozed himself out of the panelling,

smiling his most horrible smile. He made his way down the hall, scattering the shadows as he went.

The Canterville Ghost was back, and how! A few waves of his rusty dagger and he felt like the King of Ghosts, the Emperor of Spooks.

He stopped outside Washington's room. The wind blew his straggly grey hair about his head. His moth-eaten clothes rustled, all mouldy and clammy. It was time! He put his claw upon the doorknob. Then...something made him turn.

Horror of horrors! He fell back, covering his face, daring only to peek out quickly behind his fingers.

In the hall, in front of him, stood a monstrous *thing*. Its head was bald and shining, its face pale. Its mouth twisted in a horrible grin. Around its neck hung a placard, where some awful words were written – who knows what! And in its left hand it waved a gleaming sword. A rival ghost!

Sir Simon had never seen another ghost before. He was terrified. This ghost had it in for him, he was sure of that. Whatever terrible message was written on that placard, it was meant for the Canterville Ghost.

He tore down the hall, dropping his dagger in one of Mr Otis's boots. Stumbling up the stairs, he whisked through the panelling and landed with a bump on the other side. Then he lay there, stunned, trying to work out what had happened.

He had terrorised this house for over three hundred years. He had driven strong men and women mad with fear. Only a few minutes ago, he was the King of Ghosts, the Emperor of Spooks. But now, he was a quivering wreck. He felt deeply ashamed.

A little voice inside him was saying: Sir Simon de Canterville, you are a *coward*! This horrid thought was enough to bring back some of his old courage. He would seek out his rival and drive him out. Trespasser! Squatter!

There was only room for one ghost in
Canterville Chase.

CHAPTER 7

Hugo, the Headless Hungarian

Georgie couldn't stop laughing. This meant Harry couldn't stop laughing, either.

'You should have *seen* his face!' yelled Georgie.

'His *face*!' laughed Harry.

'He was scared witless!'

Virginia thought they were being mean. 'Boys,' she said. 'That poor ghost. Haven't you teased him enough?'

'He was trying to scare *us!* Fair's fair,' said Georgie.

'Fair is fair,' said Harry.

Virginia scowled. It was bad enough having

one nine-year-old brother. Twins were the end. You had to hear every silly thing twice.

Mr Otis put down his newspaper. 'The Otis family,' he said, 'must look after itself. But I will not put up with bullying.'

'I agree,' said Mother, spooning treacle onto her toast. 'Boys, you are to leave the Canterville Ghost *alone*. If there is any funny business, your father and I will deal with it.'

Georgie pulled a face. So did Harry.

Virginia went into the library to look at that morning's stain. It wasn't there! She felt rather sad, and secretly hoped it would come back. Breakfast wouldn't be quite the same without it.

Washington was thrilled. He held up the bottle. 'Good timing! Look, that's the last of the Potts'!'

Virginia wandered into the garden thinking about the ghost. It couldn't be much fun being a ghost. It must be very lonely, hanging around the same place for hundreds of years with no one to talk to. Still, this Sir Simon whatever-his-name-was, had done something pretty terrible – even if it was a long time ago. Maybe he deserved it.

Virginia could hear the twins whooping and yelling. Georgie was shouting that the three of them should have a game. But his sister wasn't in the mood.

'You two play,' she said, 'and remember what Ma and Pa said. No more bullying our ghost, understood?'

'Yes, understood,' said Georgie.

'Understood,' came the echo from Harry.

Sir Simon de Canterville was not feeling sorry for himself at that moment. He was looking for the rival ghost from the night before. He had even made up a little speech. Sir Simon was going to tell this newcomer that he had better find his own place to haunt. This was Canterville Chase and the only proper ghost was a de Canterville. So he'd better whoosh off if he knew what was good for him.

However, if the new ghost got difficult, Sir Simon had a back-up plan. He would offer to *share* the haunting. Two ghosts would be better than one, especially when those horrible twins were around.

When he reached the spot where he had last seen the ghost, a terrible sight met his eyes. Something awful had happened. The ghost was leaning against the wall, as if in pain. The gleaming sword had fallen from his hand.

For a second he felt sorry for him. Then he took a deep breath. 'Canterville! Pull yourself together!' he muttered. Even so, he couldn't leave a fellow ghost like that. He reached out and tried to lift him up. But to Sir Simon's horror, the ghost's head fell off! It rolled across the floor and his body fell to pieces in Sir Simon's arms.

Sir Simon was holding a white cotton sheet! He grabbed at the placard, which had hung around the ghost's neck. It read:

Ye Oldy Ghostie and All Uther Reel Spooks
BEWARE OF FAKES!

Tricked! Worst of all, *made a fool of!* And by a pair of nine-year-olds who couldn't even spell.

This was not playing fair. He ground his teeth and muttered the rudest, angriest things he could think of. Something had to be done and quickly.

The problem was, all this was having a bad effect on Sir Simon. He had the jitters. The slightest noise made him jump. He kept to his room for three whole days, going over things in his mind. By then, he had given up on the stain. If this rotten American family didn't know first-class British haunting, then they didn't deserve it. And that Washington and his cleaning habits! Odd in such a young man. Peculiar, even. This family were *not worth* haunting.

There was also something they could never know or hope to understand. It was 'The Ghosts' Charter'. This was something Sir Simon took very seriously. He *had* to haunt at least once a week, as well as doing Chain Rattling Duty once a month. There was no way he could escape these duties and keep his honour. That was a fact.

For the next few weeks he carried out his work as usual. However, he *crept*, he *flitted*, he *hid* under a long black cloak. And he even tried out the hateful Potts' All-Purpose on his chains (it worked quite well, actually). In fact, he left the Otises alone. But the boys did not leave *him* alone. Not a bit of it.

They stretched strings across the stairs to trip him up. A butter slide (a horrible invention) sent him skating down the hall on his bottom at full speed. He crashed into a washing basket,

sending the clothes flying. Something fell on his head. He reached up and pulled it down. Knickers! Oh, the shame of it! He was holding a huge pair of Mrs Umney's Sunday best.

After a few more of these tricks, he began to get angry. He wanted revenge. He was the Canterville Ghost, he reminded himself. He would *not* be made a fool of. He would not!

It was then he remembered Hugo, the Headless Hungarian. He hadn't used that for seventy years. He wasn't even sure he could

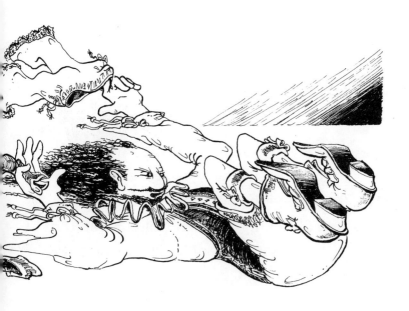

find the outfit. It had so terrified the fourth Lord Canterville that he and his whole family fled the house. Sir Simon had hidden it away in case he had no one left to haunt. Why hadn't he thought of it before?

He found the Hugo outfit in the back of his room. It took three full hours to get ready. But it was worth it. No ghost on earth could hope to look so spine-chilling, he was sure of that. The boots were slightly too big, and he could only find one of the two swords, but the overall effect was spectacular.

At ten-past midnight, he oozed out of the panelling and glided along the hall until he reached the twins' room. The door was open just a little. What luck, he thought. He flung it open…

A bucket of icy cold water shot over him like a tidal wave. He was soaked. Drenched. Wet through to the bone. Then came the laughter. Shrieking nine-year-old laughter. He fled back to his room as if he was being chased by a pack of wild dogs.

◆◆◆

Sir Simon was finished, reduced to a quivering
jelly. Muttering, 'Woe is me! I give up, I give
in!' he did indeed give up hope. He was laid up
with a dreadful cold, snuffling and sneezing,
coughing and wheezing. His shame could not
have been more complete.

CHAPTER 8

Can't anyone help you?

The boys got a good telling-off. The clattering and shrieking had woken the whole house. They had to own up to teasing Sir Simon, and Mr Otis sent them to their room for three whole days as a punishment.

Poor Mrs Umney was so shaken she locked herself in her room and wouldn't come out. 'My nerves can't take it!' she said.

For the next few days, there was no sign of the Canterville Ghost.

'He's gone,' said Washington. 'He's run away. And good riddance.'

'I do believe you're right,' said his father.

'I shall write to Lord Canterville at once and tell him.'

But Virginia was not so sure. Perhaps the poor chap was hiding somewhere, shivering with cold. He probably hadn't even got a towel to dry himself off.

On the other hand, she was hoping he would keep out of the way for a few more days. Things were changing. Now that her mother believed that they had a spook-free house, she'd decided to hold a big party. Everyone had been invited, including the young Duke of Cheshire who was going to stay overnight. He had become a good friend. The last thing Virginia wanted was for him to be woken in the night by some clammy spook looming all over him. She'd never see him again.

To her relief, the week passed by with no hauntings at all – not a squeak. The library was even free of the stain. All seemed well.

The day after the party, the duke and Virginia went out riding. He was a brilliant horseman, and she found herself thinking what a wonderful thing it was to be such friends. Then, when jumping through a hedge, she ripped her riding breeches badly. She made an excuse and galloped home. She wanted to change into another pair and get back to the duke as soon as possible. To save time, she used the back staircase.*

As she ran past the old tapestry chamber, she thought she heard someone. She peeped inside. She couldn't believe what she was seeing. There was Sir Simon, sitting by the window, his head resting on his hand and his grey hair looped around his pale face. He looked sad and depressed, and he clearly had no idea she was there.

She wanted to run. But he looked so lonely, so deeply sad, that she found herself speaking. 'It's you!' she said, taking care that she could make a run for it, if she had to. 'I'm sorry you're sad. But my brothers are going back to school tomorrow. So if you behave yourself, no one will bother you any more.'

He turned. His voice was low and quivery. 'It's no use asking me to behave myself. Quite ridiculous. I *must* rattle my chains. I *must* groan and flit about at night. I have no choice. It's the only reason I have for being here at all.'

Virginia could hardly believe she was talking to a ghost. But no, there he was.

'It's *not* a reason for being here,' she said gently. 'You have been very wicked. Mrs Umney told us of your cruel deed to your poor wife.'

'Well, yes,' he replied, stroking his wispy beard. 'But that was a long time ago. Hundreds of years.'

'It's a terrible thing to kill anyone,' she said. 'At any time.'

'Well, you didn't know her!' he hissed. 'She was awful. She was always making me look a complete fool. She made me a doublet that came down to my knees. She cooked the most horrible meals. I do believe she was trying to poison me. Anyway, I didn't mean to kill her. It was an accident.'

'Hmm,' said Virginia severely. 'I don't believe you.'

Sir Simon looked shifty. 'She slipped on a fish head and fell on my sword. But her brothers shouldn't have locked me up, either! I starved to death.'

'Oh, poor ghost! Are you hungry?' cried Virginia. 'I can fetch you a sandwich from the kitchen.'

'No, thank you,' he replied. 'Ghosts don't eat. But it's kind of you to ask. You are much nicer than the rest of your horrible, rude and dishonest family.'

'Stop! It is *you* who are dishonest. You stole from my paintbox to make that stain in the library. I recognised the colours! I ran out of the green and I couldn't finish my painting. Whoever heard of green blood anyway!'

Sir Simon stared at the floor, looking sheepish. 'What was I to do?' he grumbled. 'It's difficult to get real blood these days. Anyway, it was your brother's fault with his stupid Potts' Clean-Away. I don't see why I shouldn't use your paints.'

'That's it!' said Virginia. 'Goodbye! I'm going to ask Dad to get the twins another week's holiday. You're impossible. You could at least say sorry.'

'Don't go,' he said. 'Please! If only you knew. I am *so* lonely and unhappy. I am really sorry for everything I did. I didn't mean to kill my wife. I really didn't. And I'm sorry about the paints...and the other things.' He added, 'All I want to do now is go to sleep. And I cannot. I haven't slept for three hundred years. I am so very tired.' He began to wail.

'Don't get upset,' said Virginia, daring to go a little closer. 'Is there no place you can sleep?'

'Far away beyond the woods,' he said, looking wistfully out of the window, 'there is a little garden. The grass is long and deep and scattered with lovely little white flowers, like stars. A nightingale sings all night long while the yew tree spreads its arms over the sleepers.'

Tears came into Virginia's eyes. 'You mean the graveyard,' she said.

'Yes,' replied the ghost. 'It must be so wonderful to lie in the soft brown earth. So comfortable. Not to have to flit around being the Canterville Ghost for ever. Forced to screech and cackle and rattle my chains. Never able to sleep. Never even to have one friend.'

By this time, tears were pouring down Virginia's face. What a long, lonely, three hundred years. 'Can't anyone help you?' she said.

'You know something,' he said. '*You* could help.'

Virginia felt suddenly scared.

'You can help me, because you are good. And kind. Good is stronger than evil. That is one thing I know.'

She shuddered. She felt as if she was in some awful dream.

'You know what is written on the library window? It's the Canterville Prophecy.'*

'Yes, we've all read it. I know it by heart.'

Virginia spoke the funny old words:

'*When a kind and true young heart*
Can tell the good from the evil part,
When that same heart sheds a tear
And the dead tree fruit does bear,
Then all in this house shall be still,
And peace shall come to Canterville.
What does that mean?'

'It means that if a kind young person sheds a tear for me because I can't cry myself, and is good where I am most definitely not good, there is hope for me. *They* will be merciful!'

Virginia had a funny feeling. Really weird. It felt as if she had a chance to do something *very* important. But she didn't like the sound of this 'they' – whoever they were.

'You see, you have already done part of it. You cried for me, because you were sorry that I can't save myself,' said the Canterville Ghost. 'But now you must ask for mercy for poor old Canterville. It won't be easy. You will see horrible shapes in the darkness. Wicked voices will whisper in your ear. But nothing will harm you – trust me. Nothing *can* harm you.'

'I will do it!' Virginia said quickly before she could have time to change her mind. The words just came out. 'I will ask them for mercy for you.'

Sir Simon jumped up with joy. Bending down on one knee he kissed her hand. 'Thank you.'

Then the wall slowly faded away, like mist. A big, black cavern opened up in front of Virginia. Bitter cold, like the iciest winter wind, swept around the room. Bravely, she set out to plead for forgiveness for Sir Simon.

CHAPTER 9

Missing

The family was very worried when Virginia did not turn up at teatime. Worry turned to fear as the hours went on. They searched every room in the house. Then Mr Otis, Washington and the duke searched the countryside around. No one had seen Virginia or heard of her since she left the duke.

Suspicion even fell on the travellers that had been camping in Darkfell Hollow. But the travellers were good fellows, and they were so upset at the news of Virginia's disappearance that they joined in the search too. Mr Otis and the boys and half the village trudged far and wide with lanterns, searching everywhere. The young Duke of Cheshire was wild with despair and galloped hither and thither, despite Mr Otis's fears for his safety.

By the evening, everyone was truly frightened, for no trace of the missing girl could be found.

Her mother lay on the sofa weeping. 'My poor child!' she wailed. 'What can have happened?'

Mrs Umney mopped Mrs Otis's forehead.

'*Oh, woe! Oh woe!*

Perhaps we shall never know,' she muttered. This didn't help matters very much.

The young duke wanted to go on searching all night long, but everyone was worn out. Mr Otis insisted they should have something to eat. It was important to keep up their strength, he said. Supper was ordered.

It was a sad and gloomy meal. Hardly anyone spoke. Even the twins were silent. Mr Otis said that first thing in the morning they would telegraph Scotland Yard[*] for their top detectives to be sent down without delay.

Just as they were going out of the dining
room, midnight struck on the big hall clock. Its
chimes echoed around the house, and when
the last stroke sounded there was a deafening
crash. This was followed by a sudden, shrill
cry. A crack of thunder shook the house to its
foundations and a strain of weird, unearthly
music floated on the air.

Mrs Umney clutched at Mother.

'Oh, doom!' Oh, doom!' she cried.

'Something amiss is in the room.'

They all looked up. All of a sudden, a panel
at the top of the stairs flew open.

Virginia stepped out smiling. In her
hand she was holding a little box.

Mrs Otis leaped up the stairs and held her
daughter tightly in her arms. Then they all fell
upon Virginia, kissing and hugging.

'My goodness, child! Where on earth have
you been?' cried her father, rather crossly.
'We've been half mad with worry.' He thought
she'd been playing some stupid trick and he
was so glad to see her it made him angry.

'Don't be angry, Dad,' said Virginia. 'I met
Sir Simon – the Ghost of the Cantervilles. He
told me that he had been wicked, but that he

was very sorry for everything. And he asked me to ask for forgiveness for him. So I did. He's now at rest for ever. And look, he gave me this box of jewels.'

They stared at her as if she'd gone mad. Mrs Umney looked as if she might faint clean away.

'Come with me,' said Virginia. 'I'll show you.'

She led them through the door in the panelling and down a narrow, secret passage. Washington lit the way with a candle. They came to a big oak door, studded with rusty nails. When Washington touched it, it swung open.

They were in a little, low room with one tiny barred window. In the wall was a heavy iron ring. Chained to it was a skeleton, lying on the stone floor. Everyone stared at the strange scene in wonder.

The twins looked out of the little window. 'So *this* is where he was hiding,' said Georgie.

'He was hiding *here*!' said Harry.

'And look, in the garden, that old dead pear tree has come to life!' cried Georgie. 'I can see the flowers!'

'He has been forgiven, poor chap,' said Virginia gravely.

'You are an angel!' said the Duke of Cheshire.

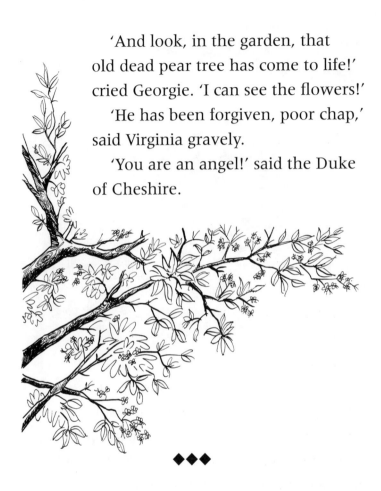

◆◆◆

Eight black horses, each with a headdress of magnificent ostrich feathers, pulled Sir Simon's funeral carriage. It was a magnificent scene.

Lord Canterville himself was the chief
mourner, having come from Wales for
the funeral. He sat in the front carriage
with Virginia and her father. Mrs Otis and
Washington and the twins were in the next
one. In the last carriage sat Mrs Umney.
Everyone felt that she had been terrified
for so long, she had the right to see he was
finally at rest.

'*By ear of pig and tooth of hound,*
he'll lie for ever underground,'
she muttered over and over again.

The Canterville Ghost was buried under the biggest yew tree in the graveyard. Its branches spread like cradling arms over the earth.

Mr Otis wanted the casket of jewels to go back to the Canterville family. Virginia agreed with him. But Lord Canterville would have none of it. 'Sir,' he said, 'your brave child has saved the soul of Sir Simon de Canterville. My family is very grateful for her courage. Sir Simon gave her the jewels and they are clearly hers. If I were heartless enough to take them, I do believe that wicked old fellow would be back to his tricks in a fortnight!'

A few years later Virginia wore the jewels at her wedding to the Duke of Cheshire. On the day after their honeymoon they drove down to Canterville Chase. It was a brilliant, sunny afternoon as they walked down the leafy, narrow lanes to the little graveyard. The gravestone was very plain. It simply had Sir Simon's initials and the verse from the library window.

Virginia scattered some roses and stood silently for a while.

'Virginia,' said her husband, 'you've never told me what happened when you disappeared.'

'I never can, my dear,' she said, 'in honour of Sir Simon. For all his bad deeds, he taught me one thing – good will always triumph over evil.'

And she never did tell a living soul, for all of her long life.

Oscar Wilde
(born 1854, died 1900)

Oscar Wilde was born in Dublin, Ireland. He was a clever, educated man and went to university in Dublin and Oxford. He is famous for his plays, stories and poems, a novel and his fairy tales for children.

Wilde was also famous for being witty. He was one of the first ever 'celebrities'. He liked to poke fun at things other people thought were very serious. He loved literature, culture and classical history, and hated sport. He had long hair and wore dressy clothes and collected art.

In later life he was sent to prison and lost all of his money. When he got out, he wrote a moving poem about how horrible jail was. He went to live in Paris, France, and died in a hotel there.

Here are some famous quotes from Oscar Wilde:

'Experience is simply the name we give our mistakes.'

'I can resist everything except temptation.'

'The pure and simple truth is rarely pure and never simple.'

Best known works
Books
The Picture of Dorian Gray

Poems
The Ballad of Reading Gaol

Plays
The Importance of Being Earnest

Stories for Children
The Happy Prince and Other Tales

Caroline Castle

Caroline Castle worked in publishing for many years before becoming a full time author in 2006. Her fiction titles include the bestselling *Letters of a Lovestruck Teenager* (written under the pen name Claire Robertson), *Rosie Pugh and the Great Clothes War*, and most recently *Tales of Beauty and Cruelty* co-written with Kate Petty. Caroline lives in Camden, north London.

She says, 'Retelling Oscar Wilde's *The Canterville Ghost* for today's children was a pure delight. His wonderfully bad-tempered, self-pitying ghost, the looming, run-down country mansion and the endearing, no-nonsense American family who take up residence there, offer the sort of slapstick humour and spookiness that has a timeless appeal.'

Notes about this book

Oscar Wilde often wrote stories that poked fun at traditional plots and styles of writing. This story pokes fun at ghost stories. In most ghost stories the living are terrified of ghosts when they appear. In this story the ghost becomes frightened of the people, especially the young boys.

Humour in the story also comes from the differences between the very modern American family and the old-fashioned ways of Canterville Chase's housekeeper. Of course, to the Tudor ghost Sir Simon, the Otis family seem even more strange and modern!

The book has been made into several films, an opera, many musicals and a ballet. There have also been many TV adaptations, including one in 1996 in which Patrick Stewart (from the *Star Trek* series) played the ghost.

Page 5
* **carriage** At this time people used carriages pulled by horses to get around.

Page 7
* **'A flock of crows…'** Mrs Umney is old-fashioned. Throughout the book she quotes sayings and proverbs in rhyme about popular beliefs.
* **housekeeper** Someone who looks after a large house for a (usually) rich person.

Page 9
* **1575** Elizabeth I was Queen of England at this time.

*poppycock A slang word meaning 'nonsense'.

*Potts' Clean-Away In the USA in the late 19th century many new products were invented which claimed to do household tasks easily. These were often named after the inventor. The Otis family have a collection of Potts' products, which they believe work very well.

Page 23

*Madame French for 'Mrs'.

*butler A male servant in charge of other servants in a large private house.

*pantry A cupboard or small room for storing food.

Page 27

*'boat back' This story takes place before aeroplanes were invented, so to get back to the USA from England they had to sail in a ship.

Page 28

*Biggins Bulge Armour was used in battles in the 15th century. There were many battles in the medieval period, but this is a fictional battle with a humorous name, invented by Oscar Wilde.

*battle-axe A heavy broad-headed axe used as a weapon in the medieval period.

*ball and chain A medieval weapon consisting of a heavy, spiked ball attached to a chain and handle.

Page 30

*peashooters Narrow tubes used to blow peas or other small pellets.

*baronet One of the titles given to British noblemen.

Page 36
* **croquet** A game played outside on a lawn, in which wooden mallets are used to hit wooden balls through hoops.

Page 38
* **chamber pot** A bowl, usually kept under the bed, and used if needing to go to the toilet at night. In the past, chamber pots were used before indoor bathrooms were introduced.

Page 39
* **plume** A feather.
* **screech owl** As there is no British owl with this name, it probably refers to an owl that makes a screeching call, such as a barn owl.

Page 57
* **back staircase** A second, less fancy staircase often found in a large house and used by the servants.

Page 63
* **prophecy** Something someone says or writes that they believe will happen in the future.

Page 67
* **Scotland Yard** The detective department of the police. The department is named after the street in London where its headquarters are situated.